About the Book

Wapootin was exhausted and trembling, but he dared not slow down. The young moose and his mother were fleeing from a bear and the horrible prospect of death. The cow guarded her calf bravely, but a year later things would be different. She would no longer protect her offspring as she did now. Wapootin would be forced to shift for himself.

By the age of four Wapootin was huge with full-grown antlers that made him truly formidable. Few animals dared approach him. But the bear and the hunter haunted him. They were his most hated enemies. After many years Wapootin was to have a chance to avenge himself against both in an unexpected and exciting encounter.

Jane and Paul Annixter write of the moose and its habits and the dramatic Alaskan wilderness with vivid accuracy. Their descriptions of the moose's territory combined with John Schoenherr's detailed and beautiful illustrations capture the moose in all its stately magnificence.

Weekly Reader Children's Book Club presents

WAPOOTIN

by Jane and Paul Annixter

drawings by John Schoenherr

Coward, McCann & Geoghegan, Inc.   New York

To the John Svensons

SBN: GB-698-30605-8
SBN: TR-698-20353-4

Library of Congress Cataloguing in Publication Data

Annixter, Jane.
  Wapootin.

  SUMMARY: Follows the experiences of a young
moose growing up in Alaska.
  [1. Moose—Fiction] I. Annixter, Paul, joint author.
II. Schoenherr, John. III. Title.
PZ10.3.A588Wap   [Fic]   75-10676

Printed in the United States of America

Weekly Reader Children's Book Club Edition

CONTENTS

1 Grizzly

His mother was moving and he had to follow. The going was rough, rocks and logs to be avoided, and Wapootin's week-old legs were still tottery. "Twig-eater," the Indians called his kind. He was a moose calf of the Kuskokwim Valley in Alaska, and this was June, time of the midnight sun.

When it seemed as if he could go no farther, Wapootin saw his mother waiting under a low tree. She was looking back at him, but before he could catch up with her she was moving on again. Moments later when a large rock hid her from sight Wapootin panicked. His legs sprawled and he cried aloud. She answered him with a chesty grunt that made everything right. The moose calf pulled himself together and made another try.

They were traveling on the downgrade now, a different pull on his legs. There was a soggy, springy feel underfoot and a good smell in the air that meant water. He found his mother waiting for him on the shore of a small lake, her muzzle dripping from a long drink. She squatted so that he could reach her udder and let him feed his fill.

Afterwards Wapootin was sleepy and rested for a while in an alder thicket, his stilty yellow-white legs blending with the tree stems so that he was quite painted out. He kept track of his mother's movements, his big ears working independently—one intent on water sounds, the other listening to the woods. He had not yet learned the possible meaning of a snapped twig or faint rustlings along the ground but, having been born in a pine clump, he knew the peacefulness of wind-stirred needles. And he knew the suck and ripple sounds of water as his mother waded out for a swim.

He dozed for a while till the stillness roused him. There were spreading circles on the lake and extra lappings along the shore, but his mother was gone from sight. Alone in the world, he stood trembling. Abruptly in a cascade of water she emerged, a long vine stem trailing from her mouth. Wapootin went to meet her as she waded ashore.

The two stood together on the shingle in the late upwelling light. Wapootin was rested and well fed, ready for another long ramble at his mother's heels, but she, ruminating, seemed asleep with her eyes open. Suddenly her head went high. She blew a horselike snort and started toward a stand of pines upshore. Wapootin had heard nothing but turned with her. A moment later he sensed it, too, a disturbance in the air, no more. He was all ears now, rigidly quiet.

There was a click of hooves on rock and a head appeared among nearby leaves. It was one like themselves, a cow moose coming down to drink. Wapootin's mother gave another snort and stood in front of him, her slim rear gone taut, her three-inch tail angrily atwitch. Now a long broken bawl warned the stranger to veer aside and keep going. While her calf was small, no creature might come near. The cow moose took the warning and moved off down shore.

It was still light, but his mother led him to their bedding-down place in a stand of low pines. Her own bed was a hollow scooped out of the mold and dry earth. Wapootin had a depression between pine roots within reach of her muzzle. Because of her calf the mother had a one-eyed sleep. She heard the resident bobcat wauling to himself. Later he circled their tree clump, lantern-eyed, but knew better than to try anything. A wolf howled and was answered. The cow's head went up, listening for a nearer call, but none came. Wapootin's ears were twitching in the pervading mosquito whine.

After the brief darkness the returning light was a misty white. The cow moose did not feed on the usual leaves, and Wapootin's nursing was cut short as she set off up-country, stopping at the edge of the trees to look back along their trail, her ears pointing sensitively. Her unease infected the calf. He kept close at her heels, finding this a bit easier than yesterday, for his strength was increasing. When his mother stopped again to stare back, he stopped and stared too.

The enemy scent was faint and far but must be heeded, for it meant BEAR. The cow moose did not know yet whether he was tracking them, but her urge was to get away, and fast. She moved steadily at a speed that was possible for her calf. They were on rising ground through second-growth timber. The trees in this burned-off area were just the right height for twig-snipping, but she did not pause to feed. When she halted, it was to sniff the air for danger and grunt to her calf. He was tiring and whimpered now, but the news on the breeze was bad. The bear had scented them and was lumbering along their trail. Without her calf she might easily have outdistanced this major enemy; as it was she must contrive to outwit him.

The cow made an oblique turn among the stubbly trees, making tracks through the thick growth to an opening among rocks. With a bound of her strong, agile legs she cleared a boulder and climbed a further rock. Wapootin bawled with dismay but was heartened by a grunt from his mother. Moments later she rejoined him and they retraced their way through the brush and trees to another clear rocky place, where she let him rest before starting off again. The pattern of tracks they had left would confuse and delay the enemy.

Now his mother was leading him up-trail at a rocking gait that kept him panting. Wapootin seemed to have known this threat before, a blood memory full of fear. When his mother paused on an outcrop to look back, he clambered up beside her. The cow could not see well, but her ears and nose were very keen. She was able to detect the enemy's movements and sensed his growing determination to overtake them and have her calf. He had puzzled out the mixed trail and now was coming at a faster pace. The cow knew by the smell of him that this was GRIZZLY, slayer of many of her kind, and fear drove her.

Their tracker was like a boulder rolling up hill. He was a bald face grizzly, hungry for fresh meat. The quarry's twisted trail had angered him and his will to kill had sharpened. From time to time he half rose, one great forearm lifted, then plunged forward again with a savage *cough-cough*.

The cow heard these sounds. The bear was still a mile behind them, but her calf was exhausted. She stopped, casting about for some possible refuge or means of throwing the enemy off trail. Wapootin, trembling, leaned against her foreleg. She gave him a hurried lick or two, then grunted an order to follow. Their best chance was a stony ridge that angled upward. She must find some crevice narrow and safe for her calf to hide in while she made her stand against the enemy. She led off at a tangent among the higher rocks.

Their way grew bare of growth, a spiny ridge without cover of any kind, but toward the summit of the narrow rise was a point scarcely wider than her own body where she might turn and meet the enemy when he came. She urged her tired calf to the narrowest point of rock, then lowered her body for him to feed and be comforted. With soft grunts she let him know that it was time for him to sleep.

There was movement below; the cow's eye caught a sliding shadow. She took her stand on the single trail along which the bear must come and fight her before he could reach her calf.

The wait seemed long, time for her to sink into the peculiar quiet of the moose kind. In her motionlessness she blended with her surroundings, becoming almost invisible to other creatures. Many times she had saved herself and her young in this way. In the present surroundings she was like part of the rocky contour of the ridge.

Breaking from the down-slope trees, the great bear stopped, his head swinging in an arc as he probed the air for direction. The grayish patch of fur that gave him his name showed like a blaze mark across his lifted face. The trail was clear leading up the ridge. Though the breeze had been against him, his tracking had been unerring. The grizzly's long muzzle twitched as he tested the air. He sat back for a moment, jaws dribbling, his long claws raking the air a time or two before he moved on. He climbed slowly, pausing to swing his head in a half circle to one side, then the other. He could see nothing, but his quarry was up there.

The cow moose heard the enemy's claws scratching the stones. She had sensed the instant he made the turn upslope along the narrow trail. Now he was coming with relentless, rolling slowness. All this time the cow had remained motionless, so that at charging distance he still had not seen her. Abruptly the bear and moose were confronting each other at short range. For an instant the grizzly's small eyes glowed red, then with his harsh *cough-cough* he flung himself forward. Simultaneously the cow reared with flailing forehooves. Two or three of her slashing blows struck him before one great forepaw swept her aside and the monster's eye fixed beyond her, on the calf.

Wapootin, shaking with terror, saw the grizzly strike his mother clear of the rock, then the killer bear was lurching toward him with open jaws. Instinctively the calf flung himself sideways. The blow meant to bash him to the ground raked his ribs and knocked him off the ridge. Now Wapootin was falling down a steep slope in an avalanche of rubble. Down and down he slithered, to stop at last on a narrow ledge where he lay numbed, only half conscious.

The grizzly hung above, frustrated and wrathful. It was not his way to go hurtling recklessly down a loose slope.

He waited, puzzling matters out, until a bawling cry reached him. It was the sound of a cow moose near death from injury. His appetite had been set for tender calf meat, but the helpless cow would be a quick and easy kill.

The grizzly expected to find his quarry sprawled, immediately available. Instead the cow moose was moving away ably enough, her piteous cries a trick to draw him away from her calf. She kept the distance between them too great for a charge, but close enough to keep him lumbering after her. For a time on the down trail he seemed to gain. From time to time she was out of sight among trees, but would reappear and the grizzly's stalk continued.

2 The Ledge

Wapootin lay as he had fallen. Once he opened his eyes but closed them again and sank into confused sleep.

Perhaps he dreamed that the bear was there again, a towering shape of fear, for Wapootin woke trembling, bawling, trying to leap aside. Actually he had not moved. It hurt too much. His ledge was narrow and the drop below was steep, but the ridge above was empty. It was still daylight, and the silence was undisturbed except for a light wind that brushed along the stones and whistled through the pinnacles of rock.

Wapootin sounded a long, loud cry for his mother, but she did not come. He stayed awake for a while, hurting and cold and miserable. The sun was lower, but the long June day hung on. He made a few soft bleating sounds, then listened, then cried again. Belief that his mother would answer was in his listening, fear that she would not was in his cries. In all this time he had not tried to get to his feet. When he finally did try, it was too painful; he let himself fall back.

The cow moose had a bad shoulder wound inflicted by the grizzly's raking claws. The effort to lure the bear away from the ridge had been painful, and that effort had to continue. Any moment the great bald face might turn back and find his way to the spot where her calf had fallen. She had to keep him intent upon herself.

To be sure that the bear was following her, the cow had to keep within hearing distance of the predator, and that was dangerous. For, huge as he was, the grizzly was capable of great stealth in stalking prey. Also he was unhurt, unspent, while she was weakened by strain and loss of blood.

Once, hearing nothing, the moose mother stopped to listen. No sound. She was returning uncertainly along her own trail when the bear broke roaring from a stand of young firs. It was his too hasty charge which saved her. In his savage hunger the bear misjudged both the distance between him and his prey—and her agility. Whirling about, the cow moose broke into a headlong ground-covering run that took her well out of his range.

After that shock of surprise she was more cautious, but kept the trail warm, deliberately luring the enemy farther and farther afield.

The slow, persistent stalk continued. In the lingering light of evening there was wolf song. Wolves, too, were moose enemies, but this that she heard was not their trail cry; it was the familiar high-pitched signaling that meant a kill. For some time now the grizzly had been heedless of the noise he made in his pursuit. Abruptly there was silence. She dared not pause or turn back for fear of ambush, but she moved soundlessly, her listening keyed to the rear.

Suddenly an uproar of sound broke upon the evening

quiet—the grizzly's bellow combined with a chorus of snarls from the wolf pack. The din continued until there could be no doubt of what was happening, or the outcome: the grizzly was driving off the wolves and taking their prey. Even so the cow lingered listening, all senses alert. What reassured her at last was the length of time the bear took over his feeding—long, which meant large game. He would be sated and then he would sleep. She could safely return to her calf.

On the way back the cow allowed herself a few snatched mouthfuls of twigs and leaves, but did not rest. The agonizing chase had taken most of the long day. The midnight twilight, mild and windless, found the moose mother on the narrow ridge, the point of the grizzly's attack. Her calf's scent was on the valley updraft. She sounded her call and a faint bleating cry came in answer.

The immediate slope was too steep for even her broad, sure hoofs. She backtracked to a point where, with the aid of her dewclaws—small appendages just above her hooves—she could cling to the cliff side and move along parallel to the ledge where her calf lay. Every step sent a shower of rock and rubble pitching down into the draw below. From time to time the calf's weak, questioning bleat sounded and she answered with a reassuring grunt. Once when the loosened shale half buried her legs, she stood awhile not moving, gathering her strength. Then one foot at a time she cleared herself and moved on.

At last she was standing on the narrow ledge above her fallen calf. Wapootin had to be nudged many times before he would struggle to his feet. His mother licked the crusted wound in his side with healing tongue. Gradually the terror and pain of the long day retreated, and he fed.

Through the short night she comforted him, but with

the return of full light there was the problem of getting him down off the ledge. She tried to nudge him along, but the way was too steep. Tragedy threatened when sliding rubble covered his short legs and he seemed unable to move. She called and coaxed, but her calf appeared to have given up. The cow waited for a time, still calling, then ruthlessly she continued on her way until an outcrop hid her from his sight.

To Wapootin this was abandonment. His mother was gone, his side was hurting and the cold stony drag upon his legs was like death itself. The temptation to give in was strong, but the urge to follow his mother was stronger. By humping his shoulder and pulling very hard, he lifted his left foreleg a few inches out of the shale. He rested and tried again, freeing his right foot.

It was slow work and very painful, but with forelegs free and by heaving and jerking his hindquarters, he stood clear. The fanning airs smelled good to him. There were insect sounds that he recognized, and the sun was warm. Slowly, carefully, one step at a time, Wapootin made his way along the treacherous slope to firm ground, where his mother was waiting for him.

Together they descended to the friendly greenness and shelter of the valley floor.

3 The Mad Month

A restful basking time had come. The cow moose was fattening, her milk was rich from grazing on the tender new grass, and Wapootin doubled his weight every three weeks or so. The calf's coat had become black and silky, and he had humped shoulders and a pendulous muzzle like his mother and a smallish imitation of her dewlap under his chin. The wound in his side had healed. Life was good and getting even better. He had begun to nip at grasses and willow tips, following his mother's lead.

The cow's stiltlike forelegs were folded under, and she hitched along, as if on elbows, as she fed. Wapootin could reach the low growth readily enough. He nibbled companionably, close as possible to her active muzzle. When his mother yawned and eased over on her side, he did the same. Together their big mulelike ears flicked at the flies and mosquitoes.

This area of the great Kuskokwim was open country, sparsely wooded, with willow and aspen growing along the nearby river. The low trees were prime moose feeding, though grass was best so long as it was green and tender.

There were clumps of white spruce and balsam to hide them from hunters or other enemies.

Other moose and many forest dwellers moved about in this secluded summer wilderness. The moose never collected in herds like other members of the deer family, though a few bulls might congregate where the feeding was extra good. Satisfied, they wandered off in different directions, resuming their dreamy solitude. Cows with young calves might wander through, but Wapootin had no playmates his own age. When he felt playful he lunged at his mother, head down. If there was no response he continued to thump-thump with his knobbly brow till she dodged a time or two in a long-legged caper. Sometimes nothing would make her play with him. She was lazy these days and yawned a lot.

Weaning him, she tore off long strips of willow bark and indicated that he should eat it. There were things Wapootin liked better—fresh leaves and fern buds—but she kept showing him how to strip and eat bark. This was because in the long dark wintertime to come there might be little else to eat and moose calves must cultivate a taste for bark. Also moose calves must not only learn to swim but to submerge completely in search of underwater bulbs and stems.

One day his mother waited on the river bank, looking back at him until he stood beside her, then grunted to him to follow her into the water. Wapootin would have stopped when it reached his shoulders, but she kept calling. There was a scary moment when the water closed over his head. He popped to the surface and stayed afloat while his mother worked below, snatching lily stems. She brought them to the surface to swallow, for later cud chewing, then sank again.

It was August before Wapootin learned to stay under water for a brief time. He much preferred to hide in the tall grass and drowse and dream till his mother had had enough and came sloshing ashore. But one morning when he was having a swim, his mother's shadowy movements below attracted him, and he sank three feet to her side. He even nipped a water stem.

Wild parsnips and lichen and mushrooms that grew in moist shady places also made good feeding. Wapootin nipped leaves one by one while his mother stripped whole branches, running them through her mouth and nipping off the tips. When the flies and mosquitoes plagued them they moved up-country where it was slightly cooler.

She introduced him to a salt lick where the earth itself had been eaten away by animals in need of mineral compounds. Wapootin did not care for the taste but was fascinated by the other creatures that came and went at the spot. It was unusual for his mother to allow any other to come near him. She had once challenged a weasel that looked at him out of a clump of brush. But at the salt lick all were brothers. Beside Wapootin a white-tailed deer chewed at the dry, dark earth. A fox stayed awhile. Later when a pair of black bears came out of the trees, the deer and moose drew back.

After chewing at the lick, the bear pair sprawled and rested. When a lift of breeze wafted their smell to Wapootin, he shivered with terror at the memory it brought —no grizzly but enemy just the same—BEAR. His mother's faint grunt cautioned and at the same time reassured. He stayed as close to her as possible till the black pair moved into the forest.

Wapootin's appearance was changing again; his silky

dark coat was becoming a reddish brown with a lighter look at the shoulders and on the legs. He had gained almost two hundred pounds in the summer months and was more independent than before, often choosing to bed down twenty yards or so from his mother.

The lazy summer days had ended. Nights were longer now and there was crispness in the air. The seasonal excitement did not concern Wapootin as much as those older and larger than himself. There was a marked change in his mother. She no longer stood off intruders and her calls were not always to him. Other moose kept appearing. One of these actually tried to drive Wapootin off, but his mother would not permit such treatment of her calf. That bull was spurned.

Others came. Sometimes there were clashings of antlers and wild bellowing. His mother seemed little concerned about the bulls' clashes, but when a stranger-cow appeared she reared and struck at her with her forehooves. The other cow did the same, muzzle held high, and there was a sparring contest. Neither female gave ground until both were tired out, then the stranger-cow withdrew.

There were two tall bulls that stayed around so long that Wapootin tried to make friends with them, but they lowered their great heads and rumbled at him. Their antlers were multipointed, and both had long hairy "bells" hanging from their necks. The two giants were so busy watching each other that they paid little attention to Wapootin's mother, but when other bulls appeared, they were chased away with great noise and commotion. One younger male was tolerated for a day or two until his restless stamping about and frequent treble bawlings irritated the mature bulls and they drove him off.

There was a growing sense of tension and excitement

that Wapootin did not understand, but he was disturbed by it. There was still plenty to eat without resorting to bark, but he ate little. His mother, too, forgot to hunt for food.

The two tall bulls began coming in closer to his mother, but when one of them nosed her the other lunged at him in fury. Their angry challenges filled the air. Wapootin wandered off and found himself some dry grass to bed down in. Later his mother called him and they went into the woods, but the tall bulls came too and stood facing each other, heads low, snorting and pawing the ground.

Suddenly the two came together with a clatter of antlers, their great heads heaving and twisting as each tried to unbalance the other. They were well matched, grunting and groaning, each straining with all his power.

During the initial struggle cow and calf stood by, showing little concern. His mother nipped a few leaves and chewed her cud. Wapootin sampled a tip or two and once reared on his hind legs to reach a higher branch.

The two bulls parted momentarily, then lunged in for another try, their antlers grating as each tried to overthrow the other. They were equal in strength, tireless at the height of their rutting fever, and so identical that a single king bull might have been striving against himself. Clods of damp earth were flung into the air by their slotted hooves, and there was a harsh sawing sound of their tortured breathing.

The cow lowered herself on folded legs and chewed her cud. Wapootin found himself a bed and tried to sleep. The battle continued without pause; there were no more fresh thrusts because the bulls did not let go at all. It was clear that they were tiring. Their snorts and challenges had become moans and groans of distress, their muzzles almost dragged on the ground and there was panic in their eyes. But they did not let go.

The cow, too, uttered troubled cries, perhaps sensing the truth: that this well-matched pair were no longer fighting each other but trying to extricate themselves and unable to do so because their antlers had become fatally locked. Still twisting and straining, they sank to their knees. When finally one of them pitched to his side, the other was dragged down with him and the end had begun —a long, slow dying for them both.

4 Long Night

His mother went *wuow-wuowing* through the forest.
Wapootin did not like it because her calls were not for
him. Night came, sharp with frost and moonlight. Even
then she kept going and *wuowing* until Wapootin stumbled and bleated with sheer fatigue. That stopped her.
She turned to him and they found a hollow where other
moose had bedded down.

This was at the edge of an aspen forest and for a while
they rested, but not long. The cold September night was
jarred by hoarse grunting sounds continuously repeated,
timed to the trotting of a heavy beast. Louder and louder.
The one who came out into full moonlight was a bull
moose as great in size as the two that had fallen. With
head high and the bone-white tips of his antlers glinting in
the frosty light, he was a creature magnificent beyond belief. Wapootin was awed and put his head down, but his
mother got to her feet with a jerk and met the kingly
creature.

She did not return to their hole, but the sounds that
came to Wapootin through the night were not alarming.
He was still very tired and slept again.

When he woke, his mother stood close by, contentedly chewing her cud, and the kingly bull was polishing his antlers on an aspen bough. Somehow this was reassuring. Later when Wapootin dared to go closer, the bull's black muzzle descended and gave him a gentle bunt.

Wild sounds of challenge and combat still echoed in the surrounding woods. Yet wandering and browsing together, the three of them, Wapootin came to feel safer than ever before in his life. It was clear that his mother felt the same. The aspen leaves turned gold and began falling, but branch tips were still tender. The sharp air was exhilarating. Wapootin cavorted, stiff-legged, bunting his mother to draw her into play. When she did not respond he rushed ahead of the two stately ones who belonged to him, and rushed back again.

In October there were sounds in the woods that had nothing to do with the mating fever. The hunting season was on and distant blasts of gunfire echoed through the woods. To Wapootin these meant little, but the effect of these sounds upon his elders was startling. His mother bawled and broke into a run. The kingly bull's head jerked upward; then as the sounds ricocheted he pawed the ground in fury. Long after the explosive noise had died away, the moose pair still listened, their big ears sensitively turning. To Wapootin, with his two great ones so on edge, the very silences seemed threatening.

On a clear, still day of frost, Wapootin frisked ahead through a stand of pointed firs. Abruptly his frolicking ended and he froze, ears forward, nostrils wide. What he sensed was new to him, yet every nerve signaled danger. A peculiar reek came with it, warm and fleshly, somehow as terrifying as bear. The creature it came from was close at hand. In a moment leaves moved and a face appeared. He felt the shock of its gaze. At the same instant something long and shiny protruded from the branches.

Only for the briefest moment the hunter's gaze rested on Wapootin, then moved beyond him and fixed, as he took aim. The double crash that followed seemed to shatter the world and choking fumes filled the air. In terror Wapootin's legs went out from under him.

When he discovered that he was not hurt, he struggled up and ran back to where his elders had been. His mother was nowhere in sight. The kingly bull lay still on the ground, his head strangely atilt, propped by the great antlers. Two upright figures came running and stood above him. There was the smell of blood and death.

Wapootin fled into the woods. For a time it seemed as if his mother had deserted him and he bawled as he ran. Then at last he sensed that she was near and stood waiting for her to come to him. She came and they huddled close together until the smells and images of terror slowly dimmed and faded.

Quite suddenly there was no more madness in forest or open muskeg, no more sounds of conflict or mournful bellowing. Over all was the silence of impending winter. Gradually night was taking over until it was all one dimness, increasingly cold. Wapootin's coat had thickened to a heavy mat. There were coarse guard hairs on his neck and shoulders and he had a fine wooly underfur to keep him warm and dry. Surface browsing was at an end. Vegetation had frozen and withered. Snow came.

The abrupt change to winterfeed was hard. Branches were brittle. Sometimes his mother bent a small tree by rearing against it and riding it down until the trunk snapped and broke, giving them the whole top as browse.

Often moose calves found the change over to winter diet difficult to adjust to, but Wapootin met it all stolidly. He was big and hardy as most eight-month-olds.

It was never really dark. The stars were so brilliant they laid paths across the snow. Often the sky was streaked with bluish light, or seemed hung with swaying curtains of light that made a dry swishing sound as the aurora borealis leaped and played across the northern sky.

Cow and calf wandered in search of food, or rested in snow-walled holes that were formed by the heat of their bodies and the steam of their breathing. Sometimes Wapootin's mother smelled out living plants under the snow and pawed down to uncover them. When the snow deepened, she moved to a known wintering ground—a creek bottom dense with willow and alder. There were other moose about, but now that her calf was large as a white-tailed deer, she tolerated them. If there were too many browsers about and food became scarce, she sought out some lonelier place. It kept her busy, for she had three to feed—herself, Wapootin and her unborn calf.

Bears hibernated in winter, but there were other moose enemies to contend with. As the snow and cold continued and smaller game was thinned out, hunger increased among the predators. Wolf packs were abroad, hunger driven and at times desperate. Wapootin was already familiar with the rally calls and kill-cries of the pack. He was not really troubled until his mother's increasing fears began to infect him. Her mobile ears were cupped to the most distant cries. The instant they sounded nearer she started running, Wapootin close behind her. Soon his nerves were as keyed as her own to the danger of attack, and he listened even in his sleep.

In spite of all their vigilance they did not escape. It was a night of moon-silvered snow and deceptive shadows. Cow and calf had wandered far that day, at times through heavy snow, so their sleep in the alder brake was unusually deep. Suddenly the wolves were there, four of them yapping with excitement, tails whirling.

To the terrified cow moose the four seemed like a large pack, each animal doubled by its dancing shadow on the snow. It was too late for flight, the enemy would have been upon them within a hundred yards. She did the only thing she could do, forcing Wapootin into deeper cover, taking her stand before them.

At the first snarling advance the cow snorted defiance and pranced with agile forelegs. The attackers knew well what those chopping forehooves could do. They spread out and circled in an effort to reach the calf, but the cover was dense and their hunger was urgent enough for a try for the larger game. The wolves had special tactics for cow moose. They bunched together, feinting a frontal attack. They teased her with short leaps and sudden darts to the side, all designed to draw her out of cover in an angry charge that would expose her rear for a hamstring slash.

The maneuver failed. Her anger was contained; a charge at the enemy would expose her calf.

Now they were leaping at her head, trying for a hold on her pendulous muzzle, a favorite tactic, for the agony of such a hold would rob the cow of all craft. She seemed to shrink in fear still farther into the thickets, which drew the attack closer. Suddenly the cow lashed out at the nearest with a slashing forehoof. One wolf was out of the fight with a shattered jaw.

The second wolf was in and achieved a lopsided hold

on her jaw. The cow lifted the animal clear of the ground, and, oblivious to pain, swung her head in wide arcs which dropped him to the ground, where her pounding fore-hooves broke his ribs.

The smell of fresh blood kept the other two coming at her past all caution. Rearing and striking out, she dealt successfully with one of these, crushing his shoulder so that he simply crawled away. Thoroughly demoralized, the last of the four slanted off among the moon shadows.

In the days that followed, Wapootin was aware of his mother's pain. Her torn jaw made it impossible to feed, and she had little energy, a great hazard in the intense cold. She pawed at the snow, digging a hole large enough for her body. More snow came and almost covered her. Here she remained for what seemed to Wapootin an end-less and terrible time.

For food he was forced to shift for himself. Sometimes he had to plow or bound through deep snow which tired him greatly. Where the snow had crusted it cut the skin of his legs, and the forage he found was scarcely worth the struggle. Bud ends and tips had become scarce; the bark he tore away was tough, containing little nourishment. Often even bark was scarce, having been stripped up be-yond his reach, and all tender saplings had been ridden down for top browse. Wapootin ate much snow.

After foraging at a distance he returned to the place where his mother lay, and rested close by. What he feared most in his loneliness were the phosphor-eyed wolves with white fangs and lolling tongues. The long night brought both hunger and fear.

Returning to his mother after a particularly frustrating food search, Wapootin heard a crunching in the snow and saw a tall form coming toward him in the dimness. Frightened, he started to run away, but a familiar grunting call reassured him. The desperate need for food had brought his mother forth.

She led him away to the open muskeg, where she smelled out plants buried under the snow and dug down to them. There was some leftover dry grass that the first fall storms had covered. Upon this they grazed. The cow was gaunt and feeding was still painful, but to Wapootin having his mother beside him satisfied almost every need.

5 The Outcast

The spring was late but mellow, with green browse coming before the snow was gone and willows leafing out along the stream. With high sun in the sky, staying long and hurrying back, and the prospect of warm weather ease, all would have been well with Wapootin, except that something strange was happening. For days now every time he approached his mother she drove him off.

He was half grown, a yearling of more than four hundred pounds, with long legs, big feet and knees and the start of a long pendulous muzzle. But his mother had been his whole life for so long that this abrupt change was bewildering. Then one day in early June he saw a small, new creature lying beside her, all wet and shiny from her licking. Wapootin tried once more, coming in a little closer, but his mother raised her head and snoofed angrily for him to go away. He retreated but did not leave until she went to her feet, the new creature dropping away, and came at him with a threatening bawl. It was exactly what she used to do when she drove intruders away from him. Stricken now, cast out, Wapootin gave up and wandered off alone.

He did not stop or turn around for a mile or two. Then he stood very still at the edge of a thicket, brooding. There was good feeding everywhere and open water for drinking and swimming. He had adequate teeth and was fleet and fast on his long, limber legs; he even had two small, velvet knobs on his forehead. But nothing was right or would be so for quite a long time.

Those first June days after banishment Wapootin wandered aimlessly. He could be quiet when necessary but often clumped about quite noisily, not bothering to be cautious. Once when he saw a large pair of ears moving above some spruce tips, Wapootin moved forward and stood looking up at an elderly bull moose feeding there. The bull glanced back at him without the slightest interest but did not chase him away. Later when the old one moved on, Wapootin followed just to be near someone.

The bull moved no farther than the next likely growth, then stopped again to feed and chew his cud for an interminable period. Wapootin sampled the same feeding and ruminated, too, for as long as he could stand it, but restlessness finally drove him in wide circles.

It seemed that being encircled irritated the bull or perhaps disturbed his rest, for he went to his feet with a jerk and a snort, head lowered. The threatening stance made him look more kingly. Wapootin narrowed down his circles until he stood within a few feet of the bull, once more gazing up at him.

There seemed nothing better to do than to follow the old one about in his wanderings. The bull traversed much the same ground covered last summer by Wapootin and his mother: stream beds, the river, the forest fringing the muskeg, the mineral-salt lick. At the lick he and Wapootin were joined by another bull moose and a cow with twin calves. All was well so long as it remained a company of browsers, but they withdrew at the arrival of a tuft-eared lynx. Though not large enough to kill a moose calf the carnivore smell of the lynx was alarming. When a black bear ambled onto the scene the whole gathering broke up.

The old bull's withdrawal had dignity, but Wapootin showed his fright of the acrid bear smell. He gave a series of calf like bleats, expecting to be comforted. Instead he got an angry blast. When Wapootin started to follow as before, the bull turned and threatened him with lowered head.

It was plain that the old one did not want him any more than his mother did.

Wapootin wandered disconsolately along the river bank. At a shallow inlet a yearling cow was feeding on reeds and water plants. Her friendly bawl seemed an invitation, but when he moved closer she deliberately splashed him blind, then ran off. Wapootin nipped some reeds she had been eating and chewed reflectively, then waded out. He swam to the opposite shore where several young moose were standing about. Wapootin walked in among them and shook himself. His cascade of spray was ignored and so was he, but their company was mildly gratifying to him. When the group moved on he went along. There was a certain security in several additional ears and noses to sense danger. Wapootin's bear fear was forgotten.

Soon the two-year-olds drew off. Three yearlings like himself were left nipping the same willows and stripping the same bark, and bedding down within sight of each other's twitching ears. Mosquitoes were thick. Wapootin led his companions out of the river woods toward higher

ground where insects were less troublesome. But one by one they wandered away and failed to return.

Wapootin had other brief associations with yearlings still confused at finding themselves motherless and alone. From time to time he found a mature bull willing to tolerate a follower, though most of them snoofed at him with lowered heads. As summer wore on Wapootin became accustomed to his solitary state and began to enjoy the long lazy hours. He fed and got fat, swam for the sheer pleasure of it, and rested and yawned a lot. It was agreeable to him if he happened to find himself browsing with others of his kind, but summer grass, willow tips and the long green stems of aquatic plants tasted just as good when he was alone.

In the water he held his breath for a minute and a half, came up for air, then sank back into the coolness. His head popped up when a pair of white-tailed deer drank at the margin and again when a red fox trotted down and caught a crab. Once there were sounds intriguing enough to draw Wapootin right out of the water and up into the trees. It was a family of mountain caribou threading the woods in search of summer graze. There were four of them, their cloven hoofs clicking on stones —large squarish creatures with short heavy necks and small heads. At the sight of him they broke into bouncing flight, their long tails straight up as they ran.

By late August Wapootin was so tall he had to lower himself by spreading his forelegs to browse on the ground. Grass was tough and juiceless now, pond lilies were scarce and the sedge was drying out. Bark, too, had been tastier when the sap was rising. He used his teeth to scrape the bark from young trees. He had his full set of thirty-two teeth now and the velvet-covered knobs on his forehead were growing.

A spell of windy weather robbed him of his growing self-confidence. In the gusty blows his hearing was confused and his sense of smell became unreliable. In the woods the stirring of leaves and branches hid all other sounds; in the water all he could hear were wavelets breaking. Nervous and shut in upon himself, Wapootin found some thick growth to hide in and stayed there until he had consumed all the leaves and twigs that his shelter provided.

When calm fell over the wide valley once more, his senses expanded in the clear quiet air and Wapootin felt renewed. A whole new season seemed to have arrived. From high in the sky came the cries of south-moving flocks. In the moose population there was an undercurrent of excitement. Mature bulls appeared, surcharged with energy. Magnificent creatures eight feet tall, with a six-foot spread of new antlers, they roamed the forests calling for mates. There were preliminary matches of strength, an occasional noisy clatter as rival bulls met head on.

From Wapootin's first small set of antlers a few streamers of loosened velvet dangled. One day threshing about in the bushes he scraped them clean. Feeling venturesome he engaged other juveniles in brief sparring matches. But following too close on a grown bull's heels could be dangerous. Even those that had tolerated the company of yearlings in the summertime now turned upon them with irritation verging on belligerence. Immature females were given similar treatment by the cows and ruthlessly driven off.

There seemed nothing for the young to do but to gather in forlorn little groups, or follow aggressive elders at a considerable distance. Wapootin had a real shoving match with a two-year-old. He was equally tall, but the other's antlers were heavier and inches wider. After putting forth all his strength, Wapootin suffered the indignity of being thrown to the ground.

One sharp frosty day he watched, from a respectful distance, as a giant bull absorbedly pawed and scraped a patch of moist earth in a clearing. Digging with one fore-hoof, then the other, the big fellow moved in a circle until he had outlined a fair-sized hole, then went at it harder than ever so that the dirt flew out behind him. As the excavation deepened and widened, a strong male scent filled the air.

Wapootin was strangely excited. So, it seemed, was a cow that came out of the trees to watch. With urgent grunts she moved in closer and closer. The bull ignored her and went on digging his wallow. Presently another cow started toward the hole but was stopped by the first cow, upreared, forehooves pawing the air. The two females sparred at each other with angry snoofs. The bull seemed annoyed at this. He got out of the hole, and, without warning, turned on Wapootin, who had forgotten himself and edged in too near. When he tried to run, the bull took after him. Wapootin was quickly overtaken and tossed sidewise into a thicket. The bull stood pawing the ground for a while, antlers tilted, then turned and walked stiff-legged back to his wallow.

Not wanted anywhere, Wapootin moved off in the deep woods.

6 Antlered Autumn

By the time Wapootin was four years old he had experienced many changes in the seasons of his world and in himself. Some of these had been painful, but by this time everything seemed to be coming his way. When he walked in among tall bulls, he was eye-to-eye with them, never snorted at or shunted off. At his approach cows became docile, and calves looked up to him. Feeding, he could reach the highest buds and twigs. Swimming, he could breast the swiftest current. Running, he outdistanced his enemies. At sight of him wolves slanted off. Black bears rumbled, but gave him the trail. Grizzlies were something else again, and man, with his long iron stick, was the enemy of enemies. But Wapootin was a formidable creature; his size and general mien were enough to give pause to any living thing.

It was July again. The day was warm and Wapootin was down under three feet of water, feeding on aqueous vines. As he pulled at a long stem rooted on the bottom, a shadow fell across the ridged sand. It was not made by a cloud. Mouth full, Wapootin surfaced and there, slightly

42

more than his own length away, was a man in a canoe. Upon seeing Wapootin with water cascading from his great head and heavy shoulders, the man gripped his paddle and his jaw dropped.

Wapootin sensed that this man was not dangerous to him, but he hated being stared at. Involuntarily he plunged forward, snorting and churning the water. With a startled cry the man sank his paddle and the canoe shot away. From the bank Wapootin turned to look back. The man had recovered from his shock and was focusing his camera on the most magnificent young bull moose he had ever seen.

Wapootin snorted. If such a thing had happened ashore, he would have charged. Instead he shook a wide spray out of his coat and walked stiff-legged into the nearest trees. He kept going, venting his irritation in more loud snorts. His urge was to put space between himself and the man who had shattered his peace. But as he went, a new feeling grew upon him, adding to the already wonderful sense of bigness and power which had come with the completion of his growth: man—like the wolf, like the black bear—was beginning to give ground before him.

Wapootin continued up-country, his ground-covering stride slowing as his anger cooled. From time to time he paused and stood utterly still, his senses directed along his own back trail. The man he had seen on the water was not following. He passed through a dark belt of spruce and fir. There was, if he could find it, the perfect place for him to be at this time and Wapootin sensed that the place was near at hand.

He moved on and presently came to an aspen grove. Here in the quivering leaf shadows the great shape of him was lost in mottled light, the leaves so delicately stemmed that they spun in the slightest puff of air. Motionless in the shadow play among the gray-white trunks, he was perfectly camouflaged.

It was still deep summertime. Wapootin fed and yawned and stretched, his wide antlers growing heavier and heavier. He seemed to have everything he could want, even the company of other moose if he cared to put up with them. Yet there was in him a vague continuous thrust toward what was yet to come. In the midst of his deepest peace there was a stir that roused him and kept him moving up and down the length of his valley and in and out of its waters.

On an August day, with the wind behind him, Wapootin stopped short at the sounds of crackling in the thickets up ahead, sounds so careless and persistent they could only mean BEAR. Even before the first faint smell of carnivore reached him, Wapootin sensed the manner of bear it was and froze. With the wind in the enemy's favor, any sound, any movement, might precipitate a charge.

The grizzly was feeding on berries, drawing the heavily loaded branches to his mouth and stripping them. Finished with the nearer fruit, he lurched deeper into the bushes, trampling and breaking down the vines. Wapootin sensed that his absorption in the fruit made him oblivious to all else. There was an off-chance that the enemy would move on up-country without ever becoming aware of him.

Appetite boundless, slobbering and chomping, the grizzly fed on. When at last he dropped to all fours and turned, it was downtrail in Wapootin's direction. An instant later he broke from the thickets with a heavy *whuff* of breath and stopped.

For a moment the grizzly's stillness equaled Wapootin's own. The moose's presence had now been sensed, his size and location had been noted. Still silent, the grizzly eased back on his haunches and rose, yellow saber claws dangling on his matted chest as he took further stock. The small, crafty eyes flickered over Wapootin and slid away, as if without interest.

At close range the carnivore reek was intense. Natural aversion and grim associations all but panicked him, but Wapootin held his ground, the hair risen stiffly along his swollen neck and shoulders. Abruptly the saber claws curled under, the red mouth snapped shut. Soundlessly the grizzly dropped to all fours and lumbered away.

The shock of the encounter, along with the rank scent of the enemy, faded out. Wapootin moved smartly again. His stride was proud, his head was high, the weight of his antlers gave him a sense of power. He wasn't looking for trouble, but he felt more than ready for it.

There was plenty of trouble soon. The cock partridge, fluffed out double his size, began challenging all comers. Squirrels wrangled over nuts. Jays rasped. Angry snoofings came from the white-tailed deer. Wherever Wapootin moved, there was bold evidence of his own kind, the bulls restless, agitated, the cows very forward. He himself roamed without rest and even forgot to feed in the fall furor.

A tall bull he had seen several times stood brooding at the edge of the trees. Wapootin sounded a few grunts and waited for the other's response. The answer was an angry wheeling about with lowered head. Wapootin was ready, and the two met with a dry clash of antlers. There was no anger in Wapootin, merely competitive

zeal and the need to try his strength. He had to find out how good he was. Very quickly he was finding out how good the other bull was. His opponent was a year or two older, more experienced and naturally belligerent. What had started for Wapootin as a spontaneous sparring match was becoming an involved struggle.

When at length they disengaged and backed off, Wapootin would have walked away, but his opponent, ember-eyed, came in at him with redoubled force. His first maneuver was a mighty wrench which flung Wapootin sidewise, almost off his feet. Surprised and angry now, he rallied and they broke for a fresh hold. Their clasped heads rose, shook, lowered and rose again. With his added weight, the older bull began pushing Wapootin slowly backward into some heavy brush. The thrust continued until he was up against what seemed an immovable wall. He could back no farther, yet the other bull still bore in.

Inch by labored inch Wapootin drew his opponent's head downward until their muzzles almost touched the ground. For moments they remained motionless, dry leaves swirling about their forefeet from their whistling breath. The older bull seemed almost at ease in the new clinch; his head was like rock. Already Wapootin had summoned more strength than seemed possible to him, yet still more was required. The stiff hair rose on his neck and shoulders, his ears went flat, and somehow he pushed the heavier bull backward.

They were in the open again, antlers still locked, and the heaving, twisting fray went on. Wapootin felt stronger now, yet as moments passed without break or withdrawal, the long struggle began to hark back to something he had known. The image was there: two matched bulls with

47

antlers fatally locked fighting on and on to the death. Fear gripped him. Wapootin's sudden violent wrench and sidewise jerk took the other bull by surprise. Flung off balance, Wapootin's adversary was down on his side. In the laws of moose battle it is the winner's choice whether a downed opponent is allowed to rise and continue the fight. Wapootin simply walked away.

7 Phantom Cow

An autumn storm had left a world of crackling bril-
liance and a ringing stillness in which a sound carried for
half a mile. Wapootin was moving over the whitened
tundra at the edge of the frost-rimed trees. He had begun
to sound a harsh grunting call that was curiously timed to
his movements and became more and more urgent as he
went.

The cow that came out of the balsam wood was alone
and calfless. This meant that she was young and this her
first mating season. She was curious but timid, and when
Wapootin came surging up she fled. The young cow was
fleet but he was faster. Wapootin caught up with her and
the courtship began.

There were several days of devotion and close com-
panionship, with Wapootin wholly attentive, following
where she led. When other bulls made advances to his
chosen one, a lowering of his massive antlered head and
a bass bawl or two, and the field was usually cleared. If
not, a contest followed. In this high tide of his youth and
strength Wapootin was unbeatable.

The young cow was timid no longer, but she still ran away, just to prove he would follow her. Turning after a spell of aimless wandering, she would find him right there, towering over her. On a day of low sun with the last gold leaves of an aspen wood fluttering down about them they mated.

Their wanderings together continued for a while. They did not go far but covered their own range in wide circles. At last, near the balsam wood out of which she had come when they first met, the young cow turned her back and walked away. Wapootin headed on along the edge of the timber. Boundless energy and exuberance filled him, and before long his imperious male call was sounding again with every stride. The rut, as the fall mating season was called, was at its height and Wapootin was part of the general madness.

One day there was a new alluring plaint in the air. It was amorous, calling, a lure he had to answer. Twice Wapootin broke into a smart ground-covering trot in what seemed to be the direction of the call, but the lovelorn cow did not show herself.

A ragged cloud was forming a nimbus round the low sun. It was a day of brief thaw with heavy dimness along the valley floor. Wapootin drifted through the mist, waiting for her call to sound again. His bawl of frustration irritated another young bull, who came to meet him out of the whitish murk, the cow of his choice waiting in the background. To Wapootin the incident was an interruption and a delay, but he had to accept the challenge and the match was on.

For a time jealous rage and the watching cow gave his attacker the edge. Belatedly Wapootin's own rage flared, and he drove the other back and back till he stumbled and fell—a short fight and not of his choosing, but he had won it, and the cow as well. When he moved away she was right at his heels.

Wapootin's interest in this cow was slight, intent as he was on finding the sender of those tantalizing calls. There was no telltale scent or track to guide him. This might be because the breeze was wrong, but everything about this alluring creature was deceptive. Finally there came another call, not far away, filled with a soft urgent inflection that maddened him. Wapootin's head went up and he gave a mighty bellow. The cow following him pressed forward with a bawl of response, but he ignored her. He had the direction now and was on his way.

Still the phantom cow did not show herself. The way led across an open stretch toward a stand of spruce, where she must be hiding. Abruptly Wapootin slowed. Even through the heat of his ardor, warning had come, stirring the hair along his neck and shoulders. Something was wrong with the air, scents and sounds seemed false. Yet the pull was still strong; he could not turn away.

Wapootin moved slowly forward until he stood among the first trees, antlers high in the green branches. His follower had stopped some ways back. The call did not come again. What did come, from deeper in the wood, was a blast of gunfire that brought a blow to Wapootin's shoulder greater than the thrust of any rival bull. For a moment he was stunned, then the sight of a man risen from the thicket galvanized him to flight. There was a further blast as he leaped away, for the phantom cow was a hunter versed in the art of moose calling.

For a time Wapootin fled with long bounds, but the fiery pain slowed him. Growing weakness as the wound bled, made him feel very tired. He hid in some dense growth and tried to lick his wound. There was no easing of the torment until his senses blurred.

Even in the blackness of pain his alert ear caught the far sounds of pursuit. He had sunk to rest but struggled to his feet. Great extra weight seemed to burden his right side, throwing him off balance.

Somehow Wapootin was fleeing again. It seemed as if he had eluded the enemy, for the back trail was empty and silence hung over the autumn woods. But the hunter was still coming; Wapootin sensed that in every nerve. Pausing on a hill to look back, he saw nothing, but sensed the vibration of continued pursuit, too faint to be called sound. Death itself was in it.

The pain of his stiff, fevered shoulder pulled him earthward. Now he heard the crackle and rustle of heedless human feet, the hunter hurrying along the blood-spattered trail, intent on finishing off his wounded quarry.

Wapootin lurched on. The sense of the enemy's strength and persistence was overpowering. Relentless, the hunter would keep on coming till the end.

Wapootin's trembling legs threatened to give way beneath him. With what strength he had left he sought another hiding place, somewhere tree-shadowed and secret where he could be like part of the forest. But there were no shadows; day's end had a bleak gray light and the trees about him were almost bare.

He found a patch of brush along a down-slope and moved into it. In his tortured state it was as hard to remain still as it was to move. All he wanted was to sink down and give over, but he stood motionless.

Not long afterward the reek of the hunter and the weapon he carried filled the air. Wapootin heard the man's labored breathing and fresh terror broke over him, but he held quiet and the feeling passed. So did the hunter, less than ten yards from his hiding place. Sensing that he would return, Wapootin remained quiet as before.

There were sounds of the enemy's casting about in search of a further trail, but the early dark and growing cold were on Wapootin's side. When the man passed by again, he was hurrying back along the way he had come. And when the last faint sound of his going died away, Wapootin let weakness take him and sank down into darkness and rest.

8 King Bull

For days Wapootin lay up in a dense spruce wood,
watched by sly foxes and jays and carrion birds, all hop-
ing that his final hour was at hand. His weakened condition was sensed also by the bald face. It was this old enemy
who drove Wapootin into high country in the first heavy
snow, limping as he went.

With the grizzly close on his trail, Wapootin found a
narrow cavity among rim rocks large enough to back into.
It was a frost-split opening in solid rock, too cramped
below to lie down in, but with space above for his wide
antlers. On one wall of the opening jagged rock scraped
his side, but it was protection at a critical moment. The
bear was almost upon him.

At first the bald face merely squatted before the cave-
like entrance, confident that the death of the quarry would
soon end all resistance. But rising hunger brought im-
patience, and the grizzly began reaching toward him
through the opening, his long yellow claws raking closer
and closer to Wapootin's sensitive muzzle. The cranny
was too narrow for him to lower his antlers, but he reared
and bashed downward with a forehoof. The bald face

jerked back, but tried again with his other arm. In his greed and haste the bear's shoulder was exposed near the opening and Wapootin's forehoof struck down on flesh and bone. The grizzly bawled with pain but did not go away. He squatted for a seemingly endless time while Wapootin stood waiting.

Another storm had begun, snow banking around the cave mouth. Through long, dark hours the siege continued, Wapootin foodless, licking much snow for water. Finally he was drowsing in sheer fatigue. The bear, too, was sleepy. The somnolence of hibernation was creeping over the bald face; not even hunger was as great as the winter urge for long sleep in some sheltered hollow beneath the snow.

The grizzly's last attempt to reach the quarry was desultory. His arm seemed shorter, the claws half sheathed. After a final try or two, he turned away rumbling in his chest and lumbered off. Wapootin waited, then emerged warily, for the bear was tricky and might be hiding in ambush.

When it appeared that he was truly gone, Wapootin came out and stretched. In a protected spot where the scent of browse came up to him through a thin layer of snow, he pawed down to grass. Then he fed, and, afterwards, rested long in the shelter of the rocks.

The winter that followed brought further ordeals of pain and hunger, but when his wound had healed Wapootin was fleet again. In January he shed his heavy antlers. Relieved of their fifty-pound weight, he was much more agile. By the time the smaller prey was thinned out and the wolf packs had turned to big game, Wapootin was ready to cope with them.

Once a small ravenous pack caught him in the open. It was a flank attack, and the half-dozen wolves approached so craftily that they were within fifty yards of him before the faint crunch of snow warned him. Straight out across the muskeg Wapootin ran. This was a stretch of open country extending miles. There were many such breaks in the forested land, boggy in summer, covered with sphagnum moss and sedge. Now the snowed-over terrain was an obstacle course of pits, holes and rocks. Here Wapootin's long, limber legs and broad feet had the advantage. Wapootin simply vaulted over brush clumps and rocks, while the wolves had to circle or clamber over them. They sank belly-deep in the snow while Wapootin's splayed hooves acted like snowshoes, supporting his weight. He settled to the race, the muskeg flying beneath him, and the pack was left behind.

Wapootin reached his full stature in his seventh year. He was one of the largest of his kind, standing eight feet high at his humped shoulder. He was ten feet long and weighed some eighteen hundred pounds. A hairy pouch of skin, or bell, at his neck hung like a heavy beard, balancing his long narrow head and adding to his dignity. Most impressive of all, the antlers now branching from his brow reached a six-foot spread. He was a magnificent creature, but in his brown eyes was a look of smoldering anger that never wholly cooled.

Wapootin had two great hates, man and bear. If he tended to forget about them in the ease of summertime, with browse plentiful and water cool and flowing, a bad dream might make him remember. He was back in the shallow cave with the bald face reaching for him, or in tortured flight through leafless woods with the hunter close behind. From such dreams Wapootin started up with a great *whooshing* sound and threshed about in the nearby brush till his anger cooled.

At the end of summer came the familiar period of loginess and boredom, but this condition changed with the first frost. One day he forked a brush path till the strips of drying velvet upon his own brow decorated the bushes instead. Abruptly his palmated crown felt light as air and shone like polished bone. Tossing his head from side to side, Wapootin pawed the ground, then bounded away.

The forest and muskeg were alive with moose again, the bulls sounding their deep belling cries, the young males trying out their strength, the cows sparring and bludgeoning one another, the calves disturbed and interfering. Wapootin was lord of it all. Because of his size and obvious power, he went almost unchallenged, but cows were drawn to him, sometimes leaving a courting bull to follow him away. Inevitably this meant a clash from which Wapootin walked away victor.

Once in early morning, with the aurora streaming across the dark sky, Wapootin felt the rutting bull's compulsion to dig himself a wallow. In an open spot among spruce trees he began to paw at the frosty earth, using one forehoof, then the other, pausing and then pawing again. The hole had to be long and wide enough without being too deep. Making it just right took time. The low south sun was in the sky and a cow and calf had joined him. At first she stood at a short distance, docilely watching, then began to move in closer. When a second cow appeared, she reared threateningly on her hind legs. The second cow was not intimidated and a sparring match followed. Wapootin ignored all this. He scraped and chopped, occasionally using his antlers to gouge the earth.

By this time the first cow had driven her rival off and resumed her stand close by, the wallow suited Wapootin, and he lay down in it. After a while the waiting cow came and joined him there.

Unions were brief in the moose clan, mates parting after a time to seek other mates. The occasional rifle reports greatly disturbed Wapootin. Most of them were distant, but his wrathful reaction to the sounds confused his cow companions and frightened their calves. His blasting and rumbling and forking of bushes drove the young and the females off into the trees where they frequently disappeared for good.

Wapootin scarcely missed them. The sounds of shooting stirred painful memories that would not let him rest. He moved away from the gunshots only to hear the crash of rifle fire in the very direction he had taken. Sometimes, wrathful beyond all bounds, he strode toward the sounds, then stood brooding, half masked among the trees.

One day he heard the plaintive call of a cow. It was the same tantalizing sound that had lured him before, only this time there were hideous memories of the long ordeal that had followed. Wapootin waited for the call to be repeated, then began to move in a wide circle that would put him downwind of the caller. As before, he had neither scent nor tracks to guide him. He moved silently, one ground-gripping step at a time, now and then pausing in shadow with head lifted and every sense alert.

Abruptly, man-scent was in his nostrils. Soon afterward there were the sounds of approach. Wapootin froze. The hunter was coming directly toward him apparently unaware. Even with the dreaded scent of gun powder filling all the air Wapootin held his ground.

The hunter appeared among the trees, his gaze on the ground. He carried a bulky duffle bag over his shoulder and a rifle in the crook of his arm. When presently he looked up, Wapootin loomed before him—motionless, monstrous and red-eyed.

There was no time for the rifle to be raised and aimed. With a gasp the man dropped his pack and made for the nearest climbable tree. Other items of equipment, including his rifle and the curled birch-bark horn, tumbled behind him as he scrambled upward. He gained the safety of an upper branch only just in time, Wapootin's antlers tossing beneath him.

The hunter's eye fixed him and from his mouth came angry shouts and threats meant to frighten the moose away. Wapootin's response was to attack the lower branches of the hunter's tree. Later rumbling with wrath, he battered the fallen rifle with his forehooves until the wooden stock splintered and the magazine was broken beyond further use. Watching, the treed man hitched higher.

Still snorting and blasting, Wapootin moved to the discarded pack and trampled it flat to the earth. Then he began his long watch.

Time passed but Wapootin's rage burned on. The long night began, bringing increased cold. Wapootin was comfortable enough in his heavy coat, but there were coughs and sneezes and occasional groans from the man above. The sense of the enemy's discomfort increased his own strength.

In the distance the rut went on, far sounds of pursuit and combat, a lone cow's *wuowing,* overtones of a noisy clash between bulls. Once Wapootin heard a bellow of victory and gave an involuntary blast, but continued his patrol. Even resting with his long legs doubled under him, he remained aware of any movement in the tree—rustle and scratch when the man changed his position, heavy sighs and other sounds of distress. Deeper than the surface sounds was the satisfying sense that the enemy was failing, losing power.

When the tardy light returned, Wapootin was standing under the tree, head high, wide basinlike antlers lifted as if to catch the enemy when he fell. The hunter sat huddled against the tree trunk, one leg hooked over a branch. When Wapootin looked up at him, the man's eye slid weakly away.

It was a day of icy mist, and the ringing silence was broken only by sighs and groans from the hunter. The man changed his position several times and was finally lying out along a branch, hugging it with arms and legs to keep from falling off. It was clear that he was nearing collapse, and Wapootin stopped snipping some nearby birch tips to keep an even closer watch.

Intent as he was on the enemy in the tree, Wapootin missed a warning scent that threaded the air. Abruptly there was not only scent but sound and a stirring in the thickets. Some thirty yards away a grizzly had risen from the brush, the bald face.

The bear had been hunting a moose calf, but now took in the situation before him. Sensing the man in the tree, he smelled the hunter's fear and weakness—possible prey there once the bull had been driven off. Still risen on his hind legs, expecting the moose to give ground, the bald face advanced with a slow swimming motion of his great forearms.

Ordinarily Wapootin would have given ground before

this grimmest of forest enemies, but for long hours wrath against the hunter had been growing in him. Now that wrath included the bear. As the bald face came on, Wapootin charged.

The grizzly's great arms went wide to parry the unexpected attack. Wapootin, upreared, struck with his forehooves. The force of the bashing blow bowled the bald face off his feet. He rallied and bore in for the close hold which was his best fighting tactic, but Wapootin met his full-armed blows with pile-driver strikes of his own. The grizzly's long, curved claws slashed him, but he scarcely felt the pain. Avenging a lifetime of harassment and fear, Wapootin went on battering the enemy's chest and head.

Killer of many moose though he was, the grizzly knew he was outmatched, and the canny brain counseled retreat from this fight-mad bull. It was as he turned away that a blow to the side of the head felled him. Wapootin's wrathful barrage continued until all was done. At last he gave one deep bellow of victory and returned to the tree.

Slowly it became clear to him that the hunter was no longer there. The human enemy had slipped away while his fight with the bear was going on. Somehow the man's escape did not matter greatly. His spirit was gone, his weapon was dead, he would never return. Still strong in spite of his battle wounds, Wapootin went striding though the woods in search of a cow.

About the Authors

Jane and Paul Annixter have co-authored eleven books for children including SEA OTTER for which they won the 1973 Book and Author Award given by the University of California at Irvine. Two of the Annixters' books have been sold to a major movie company.

The Annixters met at a special writing class taught by Jane Annixter's novelist father. Since then both have considered writing an essential part of their lives. In addition to their co-authored books Paul Annixter has published nearly 500 short stories and novellettes for numerous American and British periodicals.

The Annixters enjoy hiking, gardening, tennis and skiing. They make their home in Laguna Beach, California.

About the Artist

John Schoenherr was graduated from Pratt Institute and is a well-known animal artist. He has illustrated more than 25 books including BLACK LIGHTNING: THREE YEARS IN THE LIFE OF A FISHER for Coward, McCann & Geoghegan. Mr. Schoenherr is an avid outdoorsman who enjoys mountain climbing, exploring caves and camping.

He lives with his wife and two children in Stockton, New Jersey.